A DETECTIVE POLICE PARTY

BY

CHARLES DICKENS

British Library Cataloguing-in-Publication Data
A catalogue record for this book is available from
the British Library

Contents

CHARLES DICKENS

Charles John Huffam Dickens was born in Landport, Portsmouth in 1812. When he was ten years old, his family settled in Camden Town, a poor neighbourhood of London. A defining moment in the young Dickens' life came only two years later, when his father – the inspiration for the character of Mr Micawber in *David Copperfield* – was imprisoned in the Marshalsea debtor's prison. As a result, Dickens was sent to Warren's blacking factory, where he worked in appalling conditions and gained a first-hand acquaintance with poverty. After three years Dickens resumed his education, but the experience was highly formative for him, and would later be fictionalised in both *David Copperfield* and *Great Expectations*.

Dickens' writing career began in around 1830, when he started to write for the journals *The Mirror of Parliament* and *The True Sun*. Three years later, he became parliamentary journalist for *The Morning Chronicle*, and also began to have some successes with his fiction: His first short story, A 'Dinner at Popular Walk', appeared in the *Monthly Magazine* in December of 1833, and his first book, a collection titled *Sketches by Boz*, was published in 1836. However, his real breakthrough came in 1837, with the serialised publication of *Posthumous Papers of the Pickwick Club* – the work was hugely popular, and transformed Dickens into a well-known literary figure.

Over the next few years, at an almost incredible rate, Dickens wrote *Oliver Twist* (1837-39), *Nicholas Nickleby* (1838-39) and *The Old Curiosity Shop* and *Barnaby Rudge* (1840-41). In 1842, he travelled with his wife to the United States and Canada (where he gave lectures denouncing slavery), and in the years following produced his five 'Christmas Books'. During the fifties, after brief spells living in Italy and Switzerland, he continued to write at a seemingly inexhaustible pace, producing some of his best work: David Copperfield (1849-50), Bleak House (1852-53), Hard Times (1854), Little *Dorrit* (1857), *A Tale of Two Cities* (1859), and *Great Expectations* (1861).

During the latter stages of his life, Dickens turned his focus from writing to giving readings. In 1869, during one such reading, he collapsed, showing symptoms of a mild stroke. He died at home one year later, aged 58. He was buried in the Poets' Corner of Westminster Abbey, where the inscription on his tomb reads: "He was a sympathiser to the poor, the suffering, and the oppressed; and by his death, one of England's greatest writers is lost to the world." Dickens is now regarded as the greatest writer of the Victorian era, and one of the greatest English authors since Shakespeare.

A Detective Police Party

In pursuance of the intention mentioned at the close of a former paper on 'The Modern Science of Thief-taking,' we now proceed to endeavour to convey to our readers some faint idea of the extraordinary dexterity, patience, and ingenuity, exercised by the Detective Police. That our description may be as graphic as we can render it, and may be perfectly reliable, we will make it, so far as in us lies, a piece of plain truth. And first, we have to inform the reader how the anecdotes we are about to communicate, came to our knowledge.

We are not by any means devout believers in the Old Bow-Street Police. To say the truth, we think there was a vast amount of humbug about those worthies. Apart from many of them being men of very indifferent character, and far too much in the habit of consorting with thieves and the like, they never lost a public occasion of jobbing and trading in mystery and making the most of themselves. Continually puffed besides by incompetent magistrates anxious to conceal their own deficiencies, and hand-in-glove with the penny-a-liners of that time, they became a sort of superstition. Although as a Preventive Police they were utterly ineffective, and as a Detective Police were very loose and uncertain in their operations, they remain with some people, a superstition to the present day.

Police officers making an arrest in a London lodging house. Anonymous sketch

On the other hand, the Detective Force organised since the establishment of the existing Police, is so well chosen and trained, proceeds so systematically and quietly, does its business in such a workman-like manner, and is always so calmly and steadily engaged in the service of the public, that the public really do not know enough of it, to know a tithe of its usefulness. Impressed with this conviction, and interested in the men themselves, we represented to the authorities at Scotland Yard, that we should be glad, if there were no official objection, to have some talk with the Detectives. A most obliging and ready permission being given, a certain evening was appointed with a certain Inspector for a social conference between ourselves and the Detectives, at our Office in Wellington Street, Strand, London. In consequence of which appointment the party 'came off,' which we are about to describe. And we beg to repeat that, avoiding such topics as it might for obvious reasons be injurious to the public, or disagreeable to respectable individuals, to touch upon in print, our description is as exact as we can make it.

The reader will have the goodness to imagine the Sanctum Sanctorum of Household Words. Anything that best suits the reader's fancy, will best represent that magnificent chamber. We merely stipulate for a round table in the middle, with some glasses and cigars arranged upon it; and the editorial sofa elegantly hemmed in between that stately piece of furniture and the wall.

It is a sultry evening at dusk. The stones of Wellington Street are hot and gritty, and the watermen and hackney-coachmen at the Theatre opposite, are much flushed and aggravated. Carriages are constantly setting down the people who have come to Fairy-Land; and there is a mighty shouting and bellowing every now and then, deafening us for the moment, through the open windows.

Just at dusk, Inspectors Wield and Stalker are announced; but we do not undertake to warrant the orthography of any of the names here mentioned. Inspector Wield presents Inspector Stalker. Inspector Wield is a middle-aged man of a portly presence, with a large, moist, knowing eye, a husky voice, and a habit of emphasising his conversation by the aid of a corpulent fore-finger, which is constantly in juxta-position with his eyes or nose. Inspector Stalker is a shrewd, hard-headed Scotchman – in appearance not at all unlike a very acute, thoroughly-trained schoolmaster, from the Normal Establishment at Glasgow. Inspector Wield one might have known, perhaps, for what he is – Inspector Stalker, never.

The ceremonies of reception over, Inspectors Wield and Stalker observe that they have brought some sergeants with them. The sergeants are presented – five in number, Sergeant Dornton, Sergeant Witchem, Sergeant Mith, Sergeant Fendall, and Sergeant Straw. We have the whole Detective Force from Scotland Yard with one exception. They sit down in a semi-circle (the two Inspectors at the two ends) at a little distance from the round table, facing the editorial sofa. Every man of them, in a glance, immediately takes an inventory of the furniture and an accurate sketch of the editorial presence. The Editor feels that any gentleman in company could take him up, if need should be, without the smallest hesitation, twenty years hence.

The whole party are in plain clothes. Sergeant Dornton, about fifty years of age, with a ruddy face and a high sun-burnt forehead, has the air of one who has been a Sergeant in the army – he might have sat to Wilkie for the Soldier in the Reading of the Will. He is famous for steadily pursuing the inductive process, and, from small beginnings, working on from clue to clue until he bags his man. Sergeant Witchem, shorter and thicker-set, and marked with the small pox, has something of a reserved and thoughtful air, as if he were engaged in deep arithmetical calculations. He is renowned for his acquaintance with the swell mob. Sergeant Mith, a smooth-faced man with a fresh bright complexion, and a strange air of simplicity, is a dab at housebreakers. Sergeant Fendall, a light-haired, well-spoken, polite person, is a prodigious hand at pursuing private inquiries of a delicate nature. Straw, a little wiry Sergeant of meek demeanour and strong sense, would knock at a door and ask a series of questions in any mild character you chose to prescribe to him, from a charity-boy upwards, and seem as innocent as an infant. They are, one and all, respectable-looking men; of perfectly good deportment and unusual intelligence; with nothing lounging or slinking in their manners; with an air of keen observation, and quick perception when addressed; and generally presenting in their faces, traces more or less marked of habitually leading lives of strong mental excitement. They have all good eyes; and they all can, and they all do, look full at whomsoever they speak to.

A Detective Police Party

We light the cigars, and hand round the glasses (which are very temperately used indeed), and the conversation begins by a modest amateur reference on the Editorial part to the swell mob. Inspector Wield immediately removes his cigar from his lips, waves his right hand, and says, 'Regarding the Swell Mob, Sir, I can't do better than call upon Sergeant Witchem. Because the reason why? I'll tell you. Sergeant Witchem is better acquainted with the Swell mob than any officer in London.'

Our heart leaping up when we beheld this rainbow in the sky, we turn to Sergeant Witchem, who very concisely, and in well-chosen language, goes into the subject forthwith. Meantime, the whole of his brother officers are closely interested in attending to what he says, and observing its effect. Presently they begin to strike in, one or two together, when an opportunity offers, and the conversation becomes general. But these brother officers only come in to the assistance of each other – not to the contradiction – and a more amicable brotherhood there could not be. From the swell mob, we diverge to the kindred topics of cracksmen, fences, public-house dancers, area-sneaks, designing young people who go out 'gonophing,' and other 'schools,' to which our readers have already been introduced. It is observable throughout these revelations, that Inspector Stalker, the Scotchman, is always exact and statistical, and that when any question of figures arises, everybody as by one consent pauses, and looks to him.

When we have exhausted the various schools of Art – during which discussion the whole body have remained profoundly attentive, except when some unusual noise at the Theatre over the way has induced some gentleman to glance inquiringly towards the window in that direction, behind his next neighbour's back – we burrow for information on such points as the following. Whether there really are any highway robberies in London, or whether some circumstances not convenient to be mentioned by the aggrieved party, usually precede the robberies complained of, under that head, which quite change their character? Certainly the latter, almost always. Whether in the case of robberies in houses, where servants are necessarily exposed to doubt, innocence under suspicion ever becomes so like guilt in appearance, that a good officer need be cautious how he judges it? Undoubtedly. Nothing is so common or deceptive as such appearances at first. Whether in a place of public amusement, a thief knows an officer, and an officer knows a thief, – supposing them, beforehand, strangers to each other – because each recognises in the other, under all disguise, an inattention to what is going on, and a purpose that is not the purpose of being entertained? Yes. That's the way exactly. Whether it is reasonable or ridiculous to trust to the alleged experiences of thieves as narrated by themselves, in prisons, or penitentiaries, or anywhere? In general, nothing more absurd. Lying is their habit and their trade; and they would rather lie – even if they hadn't an interest in it, and didn't want to make themselves agreeable – than tell the truth.

From these topics, we glide into a review of the most celebrated and horrible of the great crimes that have been committed within the last fifteen or twenty years. The men engaged in the discovery of almost all of them, and in the pursuit or apprehension of the murderers, are here, down to the very last instance. One of our guests gave chase to and boarded the Emigrant Ship, in which the murderess last hanged in London was supposed to have embarked. We learn from him that his errand was not announced to the passengers, who may have no idea of it to this hour. That he went below, with the captain, lamp in hand – it being dark, and the whole steerage abed and seasick – and engaged the Mrs Manning who *was* on board, in a conversation about her luggage, until she was, with no small pains, induced to raise her head, and turn her face towards the light. Satisfied that she was not the object of his search, he quietly re-embarked in the Government steamer alongside, and steamed home again with the intelligence.

When we have exhausted these subjects, too, which occupy a considerable time in the discussion, two or three leave their chairs, whisper Sergeant Witchem, and resume their seats. Sergeant Witchem, leaning forward a little, and placing a hand on each of his legs, then modestly speaks as follows:

'My brother-officers wish me to relate a little account of my taking Tally-ho Thompson. A man oughtn't to tell what he has done himself; but still, as nobody was with me, and, consequently, as nobody but myself can tell it, I'll do it in the best way I can, if it should meet your approval.'

We assure Sergeant Witchem that he will oblige us very much, and we all compose ourselves to listen with great interest and attention.

'Tally-ho Thompson,' says Sergeant Witchem, after merely wetting his lips with his brandy-and-water, 'Tally-ho Thompson was a famous horse-stealer, couper, and magsman. Thompson, in conjunction with a pal that occasionally worked with him, gammoned a countryman out of a good round sum of money, under pretence of getting him a situation – the regular old dodge – and was afterwards in the "Hue and Cry" for a horse – a horse that he stole, down in Hertfordshire. I had to look after Thompson, and I applied myself, of course, in the first instance, to discovering where he was. Now, Thompson's wife lived, along with a little daughter, at Chelsea. Knowing that Thompson was somewhere in the country, I watched the house – especially at post-time in the morning – thinking Thompson was pretty likely to write to her. Sure enough, one morning the postman comes up, and delivers a letter at Mrs Thompson's door. Little girl opens the door, and takes it in. We're not always sure of postmen, though the people at the post-offices are always very obliging. A postman may help us, or he may not, – just as it happens. However, I go across the road, and I say to the postman, after he has left the letter, "Good morning! how are you?" "How are you?" says he. "You've just delivered a letter for Mrs Thompson." "Yes, I have." "You didn't happen to remark what the post-mark was, perhaps?" "No," says he, "I didn't." "Come," says I, "I'll be plain with you. I'm in a small way of business, and I have given Thompson credit, and I can't afford to lose what he owes me. I know he's got money, and I know he's in the country, and if you could tell me what the post-mark was, I should be very much obliged to you, and you'd do a service to a tradesman in a small way of business that can't afford a loss." "Well," he said, "I do assure you that I did not observe what the post-mark was; all I know is, that there was money in the letter – I should say a sovereign." This was enough for me, because of course I knew that Thompson having sent his wife money, it was probable she'd write to Thompson, by return of post, to acknowledge the receipt. So I said "Thankee" to the postman, and I kept on the watch. In the afternoon I saw the little girl come out. Of course I followed her. She went into a stationer's shop, and I needn't say to you that I looked in at the window. She bought some writing-paper and envelopes, and a pen. I think to myself, "That'll do!" – watch her home again – and don't go away, you may be sure, knowing that Mrs Thompson was writing her letter to Tally-ho, and that the letter would be posted presently. In about an hour or so, out came the little girl again, with the letter in her hand. I went up, and said something to the child, whatever it might have been; but I couldn't see the direction of the letter, because she held it with the seal upwards. However, I observed that on the back of the letter there was what we call a kiss – a drop of wax by the side of the seal – and again, you understand, that was enough for me. I saw her post the letter, waited till she was gone, then went into the shop, and asked to see the Master. When he came out, I told him, "Now, I'm an Officer in the Detective Force; there's a letter with a kiss been posted here just now, for a man that I'm in search of; and what I have to ask of you, is, that you will let me look at the direction of that letter." He was very civil – took a lot of letters from the box in the window – shook 'em out on the counter with the faces downwards – and there among 'em was the identical letter with the kiss. It was directed, Mr Thomas Pigeon, Post-Office, B———, to be left 'till called for. Down I went to B——— (a hundred and twenty miles or so) that night. Early next morning I went to the Post-Office; saw the gentleman in charge of that department; told him who I was; and that my object was to see, and track, the party that should come for the letter for Mr Thomas Pigeon. He was very polite, and said, "You shall have every assistance we can give you; you can wait inside the office; and we'll take care to let you know when anybody comes for the letter." Well, I waited there, three days, and began to think that nobody ever *would* come. At last the clerk whispered to me, "Here! Detective! Some-body's come for the letter!" "Keep him a minute," said I, and I ran round to the outside of the office. There I saw a young chap with the appearance of an Ostler, holding a horse by the bridle – stretching the bridle across the pavement, while he waited at the Post-Office Window for the letter. I began to pat the horse, and that; and I said to the boy, "Why, this is Mr Jones's Mare!" "No. It an't." "No?" said I. "She's very like Mr Jones's Mare!" "She an't Mr Jones's Mare, anyhow," says he. "It's Mr So-and-So's, of the Warwick Arms." And up he jumped, and off he went – letter and all. I got a cab, followed on the box, and was so quick after him that I came into the stable-yard of the Warwick Arms, by one gate, just as he came in by another. I went into the bar, where there was a young woman serving, and called for a glass of brandy-and-water. He came in directly, and handed her the letter. She casually looked at it, without saying anything, and stuck it up behind the glass over the chimney-piece. What was to be done next?

'I turned it over in my mind while I drank my brandy-and-water (looking pretty sharp at the letter the while), but I couldn't see my way out of it at all. I tried to get lodgings in the house, but there had been a horse-fair, or something of that sort, and it was full. I was obliged to put up somewhere else, but I came backwards and forwards to the bar for a couple of days, and there was the letter, always behind the glass. At last I thought I'd write a letter to Mr Pigeon myself, and see what that would do. So I wrote one, and posted it, but I purposely addressed it, Mr John Pigeon, instead of Mr Thomas Pigeon, to see what *that* would do. In the morning (a very wet morning it was) I watched the postman down the street, and cut into the bar, just before he reached the Warwick Arms. In he came presently with my letter. "Is there a Mr John Pigeon staying here?" "No! – stop a bit though," says the bar-maid; and she took down the letter behind the glass. "No," says she, "it's Thomas, and *he* is not staying here. Would you do me a favor, and post this for me, as it is so wet?" The postman said Yes; she folded it in another envelope, directed it, and gave it him. He put it in his hat, and away he went.

'I had no difficulty in finding out the direction of that letter. It was addressed, Mr Thomas Pigeon, Post-Office, R———, Northampton-shire, to be left till called for. Off I started directly for R———; I said the same at the Post-Office there, as I had said at B———; and again I waited three days before anybody came. At last another chap on horse-back came. "Any letters for Mr Thomas Pigeon?" "Where do you come from?" "New Inn, near R———." He got the letter, and away *he* went – at a canter.

'I made my enquiries about the New Inn, near R———, and hear-ing it was a solitary sort of house, a little in the horse line, about a couple of miles from the station, I thought I'd go and have a look at it. I found it what it had been described, and sauntered in, to look about me. The landlady was in the bar, and I was trying to get into conver-sation with her; asked her how business was, and spoke about the wet weather, and so on; when I saw, through an open door, three men sitting by the fire in a sort of parlor, or kitchen; and one of those men, according to the description I had of him, was Tally-ho Thompson!

'I went and sat down among 'em, and tried to make things agreeable; but they were very shy – wouldn't talk at all – looked at me, and at one another, in a way quite the reverse of sociable. I reckoned 'em up, and finding that they were all three bigger men than me, and considering that their looks were ugly – that it was a lonely place – railroad station two miles off – and night coming on – thought I couldn't do better than have a drop of brandy-and-water to keep my courage up. So I called for my brandy-and-water; and as I was sitting drinking it by the fire, Thompson got up and went out.

'Now the difficulty of it was, that I wasn't sure it *was* Thompson, because I had never set eyes on him before; and what I had wanted was to be quite certain of him. However, there was nothing for it now, but to follow, and put a bold face upon it. I found him talking, outside in the yard, with the landlady. It turned out afterwards, that he was wanted by a Northampton officer for something else, and that, knowing that officer to be pock-marked (as I am myself), he mistook me for him. As I have observed, I found him talking to the landlady, outside. I put my hand upon his shoulder – this way – and said, "Tally-ho Thompson, it's no use. I know you. I'm an officer from London, and I take you into custody for felony!" "That be d——d!" says Tally-ho Thompson.

'We went back into the house, and the two friends began to cut up rough, and their looks didn't please me at all, I assure you. "Let the man go. What are you going to do with him?" "I'll tell you what I'm going to do with him. I'm going to take him to London to-night, as sure as I'm alive. I'm not alone here, whatever you may think. You mind your own business, and keep yourselves to yourselves. It'll be better for you, for I know you both very well." *I*'d never seen or heard of 'em in all my life, but my bouncing cowed 'em a bit, and they kept off, while Thompson was making ready to go. I thought to myself, however, that they might be coming after me on the dark road, to rescue Thompson; so I said to the landlady, "What men have you got in the house, Missis?" "We haven't got no men here," she says, sulkily. "You have got an ostler, I suppose?" "Yes, we've got an ostler." "Let me see him." Presently he came, and a shaggy-headed young fellow he was. "Now attend to me, young man," says I; "I'm a Detective Officer from London. This man's name is Thompson. I have taken him into custody for felony. I'm going to take him to the railroad station. I call upon you in the Queen's name to assist me; and mind you, my friend, you'll get yourself into more trouble than you know of, if you don't!" You never saw a person open his eyes so wide. "Now, Thompson, come along!" says I. But when I took out the handcuffs, Thompson cries, "No! None of that! I won't stand *them*! I'll go along with you quiet, but I won't bear none of that!" "Tally-ho Thompson," I said, "I'm willing to behave as a man to you, if you are willing to behave as a man to me. Give me your word that you'll come peaceably along, and I don't want to handcuff you." "I will," says Thompson, "but I'll have a glass of brandy first." "I don't care if I've another," said I. "We'll have two more, Missis," said the friends, "and con-found you, Constable, you'll give your man a drop, won't you?" I was agreeable to that, so we had it all round, and then my man and I took Tally-ho Thompson safe to the railroad, and I carried him to London that night. He was afterwards acquitted, on account of a defect in the evidence; and I understand he always praises me up to the skies, and says I'm one of the best of men.'

This story coming to a termination amidst general applause, Inspector Wield, after a little grave smoking, fixes his eye on his host, and thus delivers himself:

'It wasn't a bad plant that of mine, on Fikey, the man accused of forging the Sou' Western Railway debentures – it was only t'other day – because the reason why? I'll tell you.

'I had information that Fikey and his brother kept a factory over yonder there,' indicating any region on the Surrey side of the river, 'where he bought second-hand carriages; so after I'd tried in vain to get hold of him by other means, I wrote him a letter in an assumed name, saying that I'd got a horse and shay to dispose of, and would drive down next day, that he might view the lot, and make an offer – very reasonable it was, I said – a reg'lar bargain. Straw and me then went off to a friend of mine that's in the livery and job business, and hired a turn-out for the day, a precious smart turn-out, it was – quite a slap-up thing! Down we drove, accordingly, with a friend (who's not in the Force himself); and leaving my friend in the shay near a public-house, to take care of the horse, we went to the factory, which was some little way off. In the factory, there was a number of strong fellows at work, and after reckoning 'em up, it was clear to me that it wouldn't do to try it on there. They were too many for us. We must get our man out of doors. "Mr Fikey at home?" "No, he ain't." "Expected home soon?" "Why, no, not soon." "Ah! is his brother here?" "*I'*m his brother." "Oh! well, this is an ill-conwenience, this is. I wrote him a letter yesterday, saying I'd got a little turn-out to dispose of, and I've took the trouble to bring the turn-out down, a' purpose, and now he ain't in the way." "No, he an't in the way. You couldn't make it convenient to call again, could you?" "Why, no, I couldn't. I want to sell; that's the fact; and I can't put it off. Could you find him anywheres?" At first he said No, he couldn't, and then he wasn't sure about it, and then he'd go and try. So, at last he went up-stairs, where there was a sort of loft, and presently down comes my man himself, in his shirt sleeves.

' "Well," he says, "this seems to be rayther a pressing matter of yours." "Yes," I says, "it *is* rayther a pressing matter, and you'll find it a bargain – dirt-cheap." "I ain't in partickler want of a bargain just now," he says, "but where is it?" "Why," I says, "the turn-out's just outside. Come and look at it." He hasn't any suspicions, and away we go. And the first thing that happens is, that the horse runs away with my friend (who knows no more of driving than a child) when he takes a little trot along the road to show his paces. You never saw such a game in your life!

'When the bolt is over, and the turn-out has come to a stand-still again, Fikey walks round and round it, as grave as a judge – me too. "There, Sir!" I says. "There's a neat thing!" "It an't a bad style of thing," he says. "I believe you," says I. "And there's a horse!" – for I saw him looking at it. "Rising eight!" I says, rubbing his fore-legs. (Bless you, there an't a man in the world knows less of horses than I do, but I'd heard my friend at the Livery Stables say he was eight year old, so I says, as knowing as possible, "Rising Eight.") "Rising eight, is he?" says he. "Rising eight," says I. "Well," he says, "what do you want for it?" "Why, the first and last figure for the whole concern is five-and-twenty pound!" "That's very cheap!" he says, looking at me. "An't it?" I says. "I told you it was a bargain! Now, without any higgling and haggling about it, what I want is to sell and that's my price. Further, I'll make it easy to you, and take half the money down, and you can

16

do a bit of stiff* for the balance." "Well," he says again, "that's very cheap." "I believe you," says I; "get in and try it, and you'll buy it. Come! take a trial!"

'Ecod, he gets in, and we get in, and we drive along the road, to show him to one of the railway clerks that was hid in the public-house window to identify him. But the clerk was bothered, and didn't know whether it was him, or wasn't – because the reason why? I'll tell you, – on account of his having shaved his whiskers. "It's a clever little horse," he says, "and trots well; and the shay runs light." "Not a doubt about it," I says. "And now, Mr Fikey, I may as well make it all right, without wasting any more of your time. The fact is, I'm Inspector Wield, and you're my prisoner." "You don't mean that?" he says. "I do, indeed." "Then burn my body," says Fikey, "if this ain't *too* bad!"

'Perhaps you never saw a man so knocked over with surprise. "I hope you'll let me have my coat?" he says. "By all means." "Well, then, let's drive to the factory." "Why, not exactly that, I think," said I; "I've been there, once before, to-day. Suppose we send for it." He saw it was no go, so he sent for it, and put it on, and we drove him up to London, comfortable.'

This reminiscence is in the height of its success, when a general proposal is made to the fresh-complexioned, smooth-faced officer, with the strange air of simplicity, to tell the 'Butcher's story.' But we must reserve the Butcher's story, together with another not less curious in its way, for a concluding paper.

II

The fresh-complexioned, smooth-faced officer, with the strange air of simplicity, began, with a rustic smile, and in a soft, wheedling tone of voice, to relate the Butcher's Story, thus:

'It's just about six years ago, now, since information was given at Scotland Yard of there being extensive robberies of lawns and silks going on, at some wholesale houses in the City. Directions were given for the business being looked into; and Straw, and Fendall, and me, we were all in it.'

*Give a bill.

'When you received your instructions,' said we, 'you went away, and held a sort of Cabinet Council together?'

The smooth-faced officer coaxingly replied, 'Ye-es. Just so. We turned it over among ourselves a good deal. It appeared, when we went into it, that the goods were sold by the receivers extraordinarily cheap – much cheaper than they could have been if they had been honestly come by. The receivers were in the trade, and kept capital shops – establishments of the first respectability – one of 'em at the West End, one down in Westminster. After a lot of watching and inquiry, and this and that among ourselves, we found that the job was managed, and the purchases of the stolen goods made, at a little public-house near Smithfield, down by Saint Bartholomew's; where the Warehouse Porters, who were the thieves, took 'em for that purpose, don't you see? and made appointments to meet the people that went between themselves and the receivers. This public-house was principally used by journeymen butchers from the country, out of place, and in want of situations; so, what did we do, but – ha, ha, ha! – we agreed that I should be dressed up like a butcher myself, and go and live there!'

Never, surely, was a faculty of observation better brought to bear upon a purpose, than that which picked out this officer for the part. Nothing in all creation, could have suited him better. Even while he spoke, he became a greasy, sleepy, shy, good-natured, chuckle-headed, unsuspicious, and confiding young butcher. His very hair seemed to have suet in it, as he made it smooth upon his head, and his fresh complexion to be lubricated by large quantities of animal food.

—— 'So I – ha, ha, ha!' (always with the confiding snigger of the foolish young butcher) 'so I dressed myself in the regular way, made up a little bundle of clothes, and went to the public-house, and asked if I could have a lodging there? They says, "yes, you can have a lodging here," and I got a bedroom, and settled myself down in the tap. There was a number of people about the place, and coming backwards and forwards to the house; and first one says, and then another says, "Are you from the country, young man?" "Yes," I says, "I am. I'm come out of Northamptonshire, and I'm quite lonely here, for I don't know London at all, and it's such a mighty big town?" "It *is* a big town," they says. "Oh, it's a *very* big town!" I says. "Really and truly I never was in such a town. It quite confuses of me!" – and all that, you know.

A Detective Police Party

'When some of the Journeymen Butchers that used the house, found that I wanted a place, they says, "Oh, we'll get you a place!" And they actually took me to a sight of places, in Newgate Market, Newport Market, Clare, Carnaby – I don't know where all. But the wages was – ha, ha, ha! – was not sufficient, and I never could suit myself, don't you see? Some of the queer frequenters of the house, were a little suspicious of me at first, and I was obliged to be very cautious indeed, how I communicated with Straw or Fendall. Sometimes, when I went out, pretending to stop and look into the shop-windows, and just casting my eye round, I used to see some of 'em following me; but, being perhaps better accustomed than they thought for, to that sort of thing, I used to lead 'em on as far as I thought necessary or convenient – sometimes a long way – and then turn sharp round, and meet 'em, and say, "Oh, dear, how glad I am to come upon you so fortunate! This London's such a place, I'm blowed if I an't lost again!" And then we'd go back all together, to the public-house, and – ha, ha, ha! and smoke our pipes, don't you see?

'They were very attentive to me, I am sure. It was a common thing, while I was living there, for some of 'em to take me out, and show me London. They showed me the Prisons – showed me Newgate – and when they showed me Newgate, I stops at the place where the Porters pitch their loads, and says, "Oh dear, is this where they hang the men! Oh Lor!" "That!" they says, "what a simple cove he is! *That* an't it!" And then, they pointed out which *was* it, and I says "Lor!" and they says, "Now you'll know it agen, won't you?" And I said I thought I should if I tried hard – and I assure you I kept a sharp look out for the City Police when we were out in this way, for if any of 'em had happened to know me, and had spoke to me, it would have been all up in a minute. However, by good luck such a thing never happened, and all went on quiet: though the difficulties I had in communicating with my brother officers were quite extraordinary.

'The stolen goods that were brought to the public-house, by the Warehouse Porters, were always disposed of in a back parlor. For a long time, I never could get into into this parlor, or see what was done there. As I sat smoking my pipe, like an innocent young chap, by the tap-room fire, I'd hear some of the parties to the robbery, as they came in and out, say softly to the landlord, "Who's that? What does *he* do here?" "Bless your soul," says the landlord, "He's only a" – ha, ha, ha! – "he's only a green young fellow from the country, as is looking for a butcher's sitiwation. Don't mind *him*!" So, in course of time, they were so convinced of my being green, and got to be so accustomed to me, that I was as free of the parlor as any of 'em, and I have seen as much as Seventy Pounds worth of fine lawn sold there, in one night, that was stolen from a warehouse in Friday Street. After the sale, the buyers always stood treat – hot supper, or dinner, or what not – and they'd say on those occasions "Come on, Butcher! Put your best leg foremost, young 'un, and walk into it!" Which I used to do – and hear, at table, all manner of particulars that it was very important for us Detectives to know.

'This went on for ten weeks. I lived in the public-house all the time and never was out of Butcher's dress – except in bed. At last, when I had followed seven of the thieves, and set 'em to rights – that's an expression of ours, don't you see, by which I mean to say that I traced 'em, and found out where the robberies were done, and all about 'em – Straw, and Fendall, and I, gave one another the office, and at a time agreed upon, a descent was made upon the public-house, and the apprehension effected. One of the first things the officers did, was to collar me – for the parties to the robbery weren't to suppose yet, that I was anything but a Butcher – on which the landlord cries out, "Don't take *him*," he says, "whatever you do! He's only a poor young chap from the country, and butter wouldn't melt in his mouth!" However, they – ha, ha, ha! – they took me, and pretended to search my bedroom, where nothing was found but an old fiddle belonging to the landlord, that had got there somehow or another. But, it entirely changed the landlord's opinion, for when it was produced, he says "My fiddle! The Butcher's a pur-loiner! I give him into custody for the robbery of a musical instrument!"

'The man that had stolen the goods in Friday Street was not taken yet. He had told me, in confidence, that he had his suspicions there was something wrong (on account of the City Police having captured one of the party), and that he was going to make himself scarce. I asked him, "Where do you mean to go, Mr Shepherdson?" "Why, Butcher," says he, "the Setting Moon, in the Commercial Road, is a snug house, and I shall hang out there for a time. I shall call myself

Simpson, which appears to me to be a modest sort of a name. Perhaps you'll give us a look in, Butcher?" "Well," says I, "I think I *will* give you a call" – which I fully intended, don't you see, because, of course, he was to be taken! I went over to the Setting Moon next day, with a brother officer, and asked at the bar for Simpson. They pointed out his room, upstairs. As we were going up, he looks down over the bannisters, and calls out, "Halloa, Butcher! is that you?" "Yes, it's me. How do you find yourself?" "Bobbish," he says; "but who's that with you?" "It's only a young man, that's a friend of mine," I says. "Come along, then," says he; "any friend of the Butcher's is as welcome as the Butcher!" So, I made my friend acquainted with him, and we took him into custody.

'You have no idea, Sir, what a sight it was, in Court, when they first knew that I wasn't a Butcher, after all! I wasn't produced at the first examination, when there was a remand; but I was, at the second. And when I stepped into the box, in full police uniform, and the whole party saw how they had been done, actually a groan of horror and dismay proceeded from 'em in the dock!

'At the Old Bailey, when their trials came on, Mr Clarkson was engaged for the defence, and he *couldn't* make out how it was, about the Butcher. He thought, all along, it was a real Butcher. When the counsel for the prosecution said, "I will now call before you, gentlemen, the Police-officer," meaning myself, Mr Clarkson says, "Why Police-officer? Why more Police-officers? I don't want Police. We have had a great deal too much of the Police. I want the Butcher!" However, Sir, he had the Butcher and the Police-officer, both in one. Out of seven prisoners committed for trial, five were found guilty, and some of 'em were transported. The respectable firm at the West End got a term of imprisonment; and that's the Butcher's Story!'

The story done, the chuckle-headed Butcher again resolved himself into the smooth-faced Detective. But, he was so extremely tickled by their having taken him about, when he was that Dragon in disguise, to show him London, that he could not help reverting to that point in his narrative; and gently repeating, with the Butcher snigger, '"Oh, dear!" I says, "is that where they hang the men? Oh, Lor!" "*That!*" says they. "What a simple cove he is!"'

It being now late, and the party very modest in their fear of being too diffuse, there were some tokens of separation; when Sergeant Dornton, the soldierly-looking man, said, looking round him with a smile:

'Before we break up, Sir, perhaps you might have some amusement in hearing of the Adventures of a Carpet Bag. They are very short; and, I think, curious.'

We welcomed the Carpet Bag, as cordially as Mr Shepherdson welcomed the false Butcher at the Setting Moon. Sergeant Dornton proceeded:

'In 1847, I was dispatched to Chatham, in search of one Mesheck, a Jew. He had been carrying on, pretty heavily, in the bill-stealing way, getting acceptances from young men of good connexions (in the army chiefly), on pretence of discount, and bolting with the same.

'Mesheck was off, before I got to Chatham. All I could learn about him was, that he had gone, probably to London, and had with him – a Carpet Bag.

'I came back to town, by the last train from Blackwall, and made inquiries concerning a Jew passenger with – a Carpet Bag.

'The office was shut up, it being the last train. There were only two or three porters left. Looking after a Jew with a Carpet Bag, on the Blackwall Railway, which was then the high road to a great Military Depôt, was worse than looking after a needle in a hayrick. But it happened that one of these porters had carried, for a certain Jew, to a certain public-house, a certain – Carpet Bag.

'I went to the public-house, but the Jew had only left his luggage there for a few hours, and had called for it in a cab, and taken it away. I put such questions there, and to the porter, as I thought prudent, and got at this description of – the Carpet Bag.

'It was a bag which had, on one side of it, worked in worsted, a green parrot on a stand. A green parrot on a stand was the means by which to identify that – Carpet Bag.

'I traced Mesheck, by means of this green parrot on a stand, to Cheltenham, to Birmingham, to Liverpool, to the Atlantic Ocean. At Liverpool he was too many for me. He had gone to the United States, and I gave up all thoughts of Mesheck, and likewise of his – Carpet Bag.

'Many months afterwards – near a year afterwards – there was a Bank in Ireland robbed of seven thousand pounds, by a person of the name of Doctor Dundey, who escaped to America; from which country some of the stolen notes came home. He was supposed to have bought a farm in New Jersey. Under proper management, that estate could be seized and sold, for the benefit of the parties he had defrauded. I was sent off to America for this purpose.

'I landed at Boston. I went on to New York. I found that he had lately changed New York paper-money for New Jersey paper-money, and had banked cash in New Brunswick. To take this Doctor Dundey, it was necessary to entrap him into the State of New York, which required a deal of artifice and trouble. At one time, he couldn't be drawn into an appointment. At another time, he appointed to come to meet me, and a New York officer, on a pretext I made; and then his children had the measles. At last, he came, per steamboat, and I took him, and lodged him in a New York Prison called the Tombs; which I dare say you know, Sir?'

Editorial acknowledgment to that effect.

'I went to the Tombs, on the morning after his capture, to attend the examination before the magistrate. I was passing through the magistrate's private room, when, happening to look round me to take notice of the place, as we generally have a habit of doing, I clapped my eyes, in one corner, on a – Carpet Bag.

'What did I see upon that Carpet Bag, it you'll believe me, but a green parrot on a stand, as large as life!

' "That Carpet Bag, with the representation of a green parrot on a stand," said I, "belongs to an English Jew, named Aaron Mesheck, and to no other man, alive or dead!"

'I give you my word the New York Police officers were doubled up with surprise.

' "How do you ever come to know that?" said they.

' "I think I ought to know that green parrot by this time," said I; "for I have had as pretty a dance after that bird, at home, as ever I had, in all my life!" '

'And *was* it Mesheck's?' we submissively inquired.

'Was it, Sir? Of course it was! He was in custody for another offence, in that very identical Tombs, at that very identical time. And, more than that! Some memoranda, relating to the fraud for which I had vainly endeavoured to take him, were found to be, at that moment, lying in that very same individual – Carpet Bag!'

Such are the curious coincidences and such is the peculiar ability, always sharpening and being improved by practice, and always adapting itself to every variety of circumstances, and opposing itself to every new device that perverted ingenuity can invent, for which this important social branch of the public service is remarkable! For ever on the watch, with their wits stretched to the utmost, these officers have, from day to day and year to year, to set themselves against every novelty of trickery and dexterity that the combined imaginations of all the lawless rascals in England can devise, and to keep pace with every such invention that comes out. In the Courts of Justice, the materials of thousands of such stories as we have narrated – often elevated into the marvellous and romantic, by the circumstances of the case – are dryly compressed into the set phrase, 'in consequence of information I received, I did so and so.' Suspicion was to be directed, by careful inference and deduction, upon the right person; the right person was to be taken, wherever he had gone, or whatever he was doing to avoid detection: he is taken; there he is at the bar; that is enough. From information I, the officer, received, I did it; and, according to the custom in these cases, I say no more.

These games of chess, played with live pieces, are played before small audiences, and are chronicled nowhere. The interest of the game supports the player. Its results are enough for Justice. To compare great things with small, suppose LEVERRIER or ADAMS informing the public that from information he had received he had discovered a new planet; or COLUMBUS informing the public of his day that from information he had received, he had discovered a new continent; so the Detectives inform it that they have discovered a new fraud or an old offender, and the process is unknown.

Thus, at midnight, closed the proceedings of our curious and interesting party. But one other circumstance finally wound up the evening, after our Detective guests had left us. One of the sharpest among them, and the officer best acquainted with the swell mob, had his pocket picked, going home!